# SNAIL & WORM

Written & Illustrated
by Tina Kügler

Houghton Mifflin Harcourt
Boston   New York

# For Carson

Copyright © 2016 by Tina Kügler

www.hmhco.com

The text of this book is set in Aldus LT Std.
Tina used acrylic on pastel paper, collage, and digital media to create
the illustrations. No snails or worms were harmed in the making of
this book.

*Library of Congress Cataloging-in-Publication Data*
Kügler, Tina, author, illustrator.
  Snail and Worm : three stories about two friends / by Tina Kügler.
    pages cm
  Summary: Snail and Worm are best friends who support each
other during a silly game of tag, through Snail's adventure up a
flower stalk, and when Worm's pet goes missing.
  ISBN 978-0-544-49412-1 (alk. paper)
 [1. Best friends—Fiction. 2. Friendship—Fiction. 3. Snails—
Fiction. 4. Worms—Fiction.] I. Kügler, Carson, illustrator. II.
Title. III. Title: Meet my friend.
  PZ7.1.K844Sng 2016
  [E]—dc23

                                    2015002205


                    Manufactured in Malaysia
                    TWP 10 9 8 7 6 5 4 3 2 1
                          4500570727

MEET MY FRIEND

Hello!
Want to play?
Let's play!

TAG!
You are
it!

Can you catch me? No! No! No!

Hello?
Are you talking to a rock?

A rock?
That rock is Bob.

Hi, Bob.

This stick is Ann.

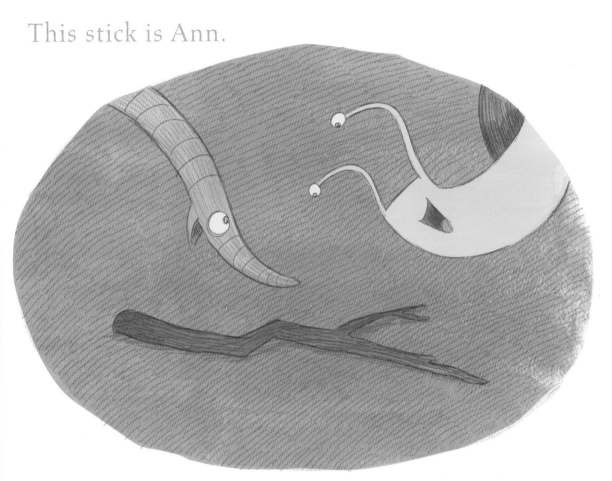

How do you do?

Do you want to play?

Yes, I want to play.

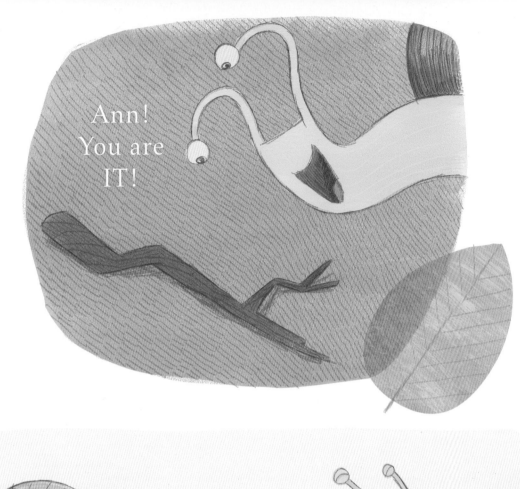

Ann!
You are
IT!

SNAIL'S ADVENTURE

Wow.

Look at that tall flower.

That is a tall flower.

I want to be
tall, too.
I wish I could
climb
to the top
of that flower.
Do you think
I can?

I am so small.
The flower is very,
very tall.

You can do it!

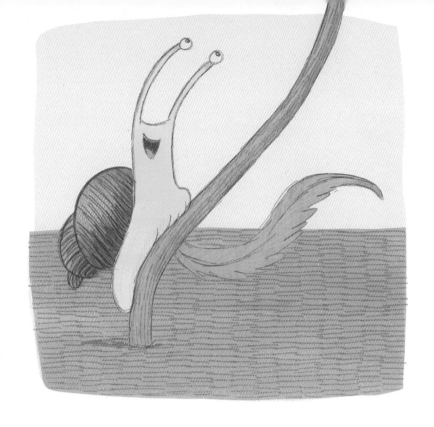

Here I go!

You can do it!
You can climb
that tall flower!

I
am
climbing!

Go! Go! Go!

I am almost to
the top!

You are almost there!

I

DID

IT!

YOU

DID

IT!

Wow! I can see so much from up here!

Wow!
They look
like ants
down there!

Wow! I can see
my house!

I did it!
Are you proud of me?

I am very proud of you.

Now

how do I

get

down?

Well, he has legs.

Is he a spider?
Spiders have legs.

He is big
and furry.

Spiders are big.
Spiders are furry.

He is brown.

I bet he is a spider!

He has sharp
teeth.

Oh, my!
He must be a spider!

Oh!

Here
he
comes!

SPIDER!

This is Sam.

He is nice.

Oh. That is a big spider. I am glad he is nice.

Thank you for
helping me find him.

Hey! Here comes my pet.
His name is Rex.

Oh.
Hello,
Rex.

Rex is a
good dog.

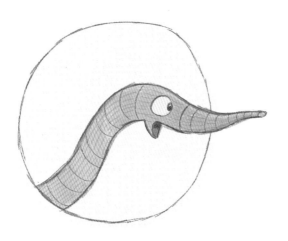

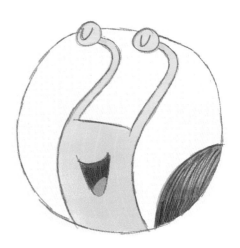

Are you sure?

Yes, I am sure.
He is very good.

I have to take Rex for a walk now.
Follow me, boy!